For Benjamin, all his butties
including Levi, Zebbi, Millie
and, of course,
Iestyn
DM

To my small friends Aidan and Noah xx
SC

This book belongs to

_____

Published in 2008 by Pont Books, an imprint of
Gomer Press, Llandysul, Ceredigion SA44 4JL

ISBN 978 184323 910 9

A CIP record for this title is available from the British Library.

© Daniel Morden & Suzanne Carpenter, 2008

Daniel Morden & Suzanne Carpenter have asserted their moral rights
under the Copyright, Designs and Patents Act, 1988 to be identified
as author and illustrator of this work.

This book is published with the financial support of the
Welsh Books Council.

Printed and bound in Wales at
Gomer Press, Llandysul, Ceredigion

Tuck Your Vest In

Daniel Morden   Suzanne Carpenter

Pont

Tuck your vest in, Iestyn.

Catch the stroller, Lola.

What's that smell, Chanelle?

Give it back, Jack.

Coats

Oh my gosh, Josh!

pryfed   insects

Blow your nose, Rose

What a mess, Jess!

That looks gooey, Louis.

Oops a daisy, Maisy!

Jam or ham, Sam?

Time to go, Joe.

I'm a champ, Bamp!